# Chapter 1

Quicksand

He was trapped in Kaplan, La. He hated the feeling of being trapped, yet there was nothing he could do about it. Kaplan was a dead end for lost souls, but Edmond had vowed to himself that somehow he was going to find a way out.

Edmond was awakened by the morning sunlight. It was 7 AM. He rose up from his bed and went into the bathroom. He splashed water on his face and brushed his teeth. He still had on the clothes that he had worn yesterday. Edmond looked into the mirror and decided that his clothes were clean enough for another day. The house he lived in was small and the refrigerator was bare.

Edmond reached into his pockets. He pulled out a five dollar bill and two quarters. Good, he thought to himself just enough for a pint of whiskey.

01/16/2015

He opened up the front door so that he could check the weather. The sun was beaming and the heat was rising. An old white man with a cane walked at a slow pace along the road. The old man waved. Edmond waved back, and then closed his door.

Edmond looked around the house for his tennis shoes. He wanted to make it to the store before the humid heat gained its strength. He found one shoe with ease, but the other was nowhere to be found. It reminded Edmond of a game of hide and go seek. The game he use to play with the other kids when he was younger. Those times were long gone and so far away that it almost seemed like a dream.

"Where's that goddamn shoe?" said Edmond to himself.

He searched. He scratched his head and wondered. And just when he was about to give up his search, he spotted the tip of the tennis shoes under his tattered and torn sofa. It was almost like the shoe was smiling at him. Playing a game of hide and go seek. Edmond snatched up the shoe and put it on.

He walked out the front door without bothering to lock up. Besides, would bother breaking into his place he thought. He had nothing worth stealing, not even a slice of bread!

### # # #

The summer heat was rising. The Kaplan streets were dead as usual except for a few cars passing. Edmond walked at a slowed pace. He watched as young men drove in their company trucks, on their way to work. Edmond did not have a job. He was three months behind on his rent. In two more weeks, his unemployment benefits would be cut off. His electricity would be disconnected in another week. He tried not to think about his problems.

The liquor store was a block away. He picked up the pace. Edmond crossed the highway and then entered the store. He was a regular there and the cashiers knew him. Edmond knew them too.

"Good morning, Mr. Edmond. What can I get for you?" asked Connie the cashier with a smile on her face. Connie was a middle aged woman with long gray hair and happy brown eyes.

"A pint of your cheapest whiskey", Edmond said. Edmond could feel the eyes of the other customers on him. He paid them no mind.

Connie reached for the whiskey, placed it on the counter, and rung it up. "$4.59", said Connie while she placed the whiskey in a small brown bag.

Edmond pulled out his last five bucks without hesitation.

"Have a nice day", said Connie. She handed Edmond his change and moved on to the next customer.

While walking home, Edmond wondered if Connie the cashier had a crush on him. He had not had a steady relationship in over five years. The women in Kaplan were fickle, so he stayed to himself.

"Hey Edmond, you got a cigarette?" A female voice called out.

Edmond was so deep in thought that he did not notice the skinny woman on a bicycle pulling up beside him. "No Tonya, I quit smoking a year ago. I told you that yesterday."

"Damn, I forgot", said Tonya. "Where you goin'?"

"Back home."

Tonya slowed down her bike and rode alongside him. Tonya was a thin woman. She could have been a beauty queen if only she would leave the drugs alone. The black wife beater she wore barely held up on her shoulders. Her breasts were small and erect. Tonya's eyes were bloodshot red from staying up the night before. She was always chasing a high. "You want some company?"

"That's up to you, Tonya. I don't have no money."

Tonya was a prostitute and the only form of a woman that Edmond had in his lonely life. He had slept with Tonya plenty of times, but their relationship was strictly business. When the two were not conducting business, they joked around like old friends.

"What you got to drink?" asked Tonya.

Edmond pulled the bottle out from the bag. "Some whiskey."

Tonya frowned. "You know I can't drink that shit. It makes me sick."

"Well, more for me", said Edmond.

They both laughed.

"Man, I need a cigarette bad. You ain't got no change", Tonya asked.

Edmond pulled out the remaining change from his pocket and gave it to her. Tonya counted the change in the palm of her skinny hand. Tonya was a woman of the streets. She knew how to hustle and she learned how to survive.

"Thanks Edmond", she said, "I'll come back by your house if I come up on somethin'." Tonya rode off with a burst of speed.

Edmond continued to walk. He hoped that Tonya would come back later, he needed the company. But for a woman like Tonya, time was money. And at that moment, Edmond was low on cash.

Edmond arrived at his house. He opened the front door, went in, and turned on the radio. He went back outside and sat on the porch with his bottle of whiskey. He twisted the top off the bottle. He took a long good swig. The liquor tasted good. Edmond was deep in thought, trying to figure out his next move. All he could think about was moving far away from Kaplan, La. and never return.

**Chapter 2**

The Sweet Taste of Blood

I have been around for centuries. I have lived all over the world, but now I reside in a small town known as Vermilion parish. Some people might say that I am a vampire, but I prefer to be called a creature of the night.

The term vampire is glamorized on television. I chuckled when I see television shows like True Blood or movies like Twilight. Humans are weird to me. I often wonder why they would want to glamorize evil? I am a soulless life form. I am void of emotions. I cannot feel love, fear, or any other weak emotions that is embedded in human nature. My only weakness is my constant cravings for blood and sex.

My lust for the female body is unquenchable. When I walk pass a woman on her period, the smell of her blood drives me wild. I hunt day and night for women on their menstrual cycle. To restore my powers I sleep three days out of a month.

01/16/2015

Being the alpha male, I kill other males for sport. I only drink the blood of female species. I can be destroyed but only by one method (which I will not reveal). I dwell among simple human beings who have no concept about life or death...

### 

Her name was Mary Andrews. She was 24 years old. She had long blonde hair and her eyes were crystal blue. I had my eyes on her for about a year now. I studied all of her moves. I watched and learned the places she frequents. Mary's period blood had a sweet smell. I could tell from her smell that she was a virgin.

Mary Andrews' period always arrived at the end of the month. The sweet smell of her virgin blood drove me wild! To a creature of the night, a virgin's blood is the ultimate cuisine.

One night my patience paid off. Mary's car was on the side of the road with the hood up. I stopped my vehicle and asked her if she needed some help.

Mary looked at me with distrustful eyes. "My car won't start", she said. "I live right up the road. Can you give me a lift?"

Mary was on her cycle. I could smell her sweet blood. I tried to control my lust. "Sure, hop in."

Mary got in on the passenger side. Lightning ripped through the sky causing the darkness to illuminate for a split second.

"I'm glad you came along when you did. This weather is about to get crazy", said Mary.

I kept quiet as I inhaled the sweet smell of her blood.

"This is a nice car. What do you do for a living?" asked Mary. Her blonde hair flowed in the wind.

"I'm in real estate", I answered. "I run a small business from my home. By the way, my name is Henry."

"I'm Mary."

I already knew everything about her. I had studied her in and out, but I could not let her know. She would probably be freaked out if she would have known my true intentions.

"Nice to meet you, Mary."

"Likewise", said Mary. She reclined back in the seat. I could tell that I had earned her trust.

We drove through the darkness in awkward silence. I could smell Mary's blood. I could hear her heart beating. I wanted her blood. I wanted her soul.

"Take a right", said Mary.

I hung a right.

"My house is there to the left", she said.

I pulled into her driveway.

"Thanks Henry, I really appreciate this. What do I owe you for your troubles?" asked Mary as she exited my vehicle.

"You're welcome", I said, "how about a cup of coffee?" (Once you invite a creature of the night into your home, he needs no further invitation.)

Mary smiled. "Well, I guess I can whip up a pot of coffee. I could use the company anyway."

My mouth watered as I climbed out of the car with haste. I waited behind Mary as she unlocked the front door. We entered her home. Mary's house was neat and well decorated.

"Have a seat, Henry. I'll get the coffee brewing."

I sat down and admired Mary's young body as she left the room. My mouth watered for her blood, but I was careful not to show my cravings. I stared at the paintings that hung on Mary's walls. I was once a painter and I knew a lot about the arts. But Mary's style of paintings were foreign to me.

Mary came back into the living room. She handed me a cup of hot coffee. She took a seat next to me. I looked into her crystal blue eyes. I attempted to hypnotize her. Hypnotism is a special gift that my kind is blessed with. I took a sip of my coffee, never taking my eyes off of Mary. The coffee had a strange taste, but I paid it no mind because I did not want to break my trance.

Mary stared back at me. "How's the coffee, Henry?"

I took another sip. "The coffee is... it's..." I felt my insides burning. I felt a searing hot flame growing within me. I had experienced this pain before. It was years back when an old Priest tried to destroy me. I felt dizzy. I dropped my cup. The coffee cup shattered on the wooden floor.

Mary smiled and evil smile. "I have been chasing you for years, Mr. Henry Von Tempt."

I shuddered with fear when Mary quoted my full name.

Mary continue, "you murdered my whole family 20 years ago and now you are going to pay."

I tried to rise from my seat, but my limbs were useless. I fell to the floor face first. "What did you do to me?" I asked as I gasped for air.

"Holy water", said Mary taking a sip of her coffee. "It gets 'em all the time."

Mary rose up out of her seat. She reached under the sofa's cushion and pulled out a long sword. Mary placed her foot on my throat as I struggled in vain. She raised the sword over her head and slammed it down with brute force. And I was summoned to a world of darkness and hell!

01/16/2015

**Chapter 3**


Love Argument


Their love was deep, so deep that they hated each other. The young couple had decided to move in together three months ago, despite the various problems in their relationship. They despised one another, they lusted after each other. Therefore they argue each and every day.


The argument usually started between 8 PM or 8:30. The argument could be started over something as little as what programs to watch on television. The fuss always boiled over into greater things. It did not take much for both tempers to flare.


"Mase, you're a selfish human being", Jada  would say.


Mase smiled a sly smile accepting the bait. "And you ain't nothin' but a spoiled brat."

Jada hated being called a brat even though there was some truth to Mase's accusations.

"Nigga, you ain't nothing but a lazy bum. Go find a job and then you can call me a brat. I pay all the damn bills!" Jada shouted. Jada knew that Mase's unemployment was a sensitive issue.

Mase's temper rose. "Yeah, and when I do find a job, I'll be outta here!"

"Leave now, Mase! Go me that bitch, Leela. You know the one who was texting your phone. The phone that I pay for."

Mase jumped up from his seat. "Maybe I Will!"

Jada was beyond angry. "I'll pack up your shit right now", said Jada. Jada jumped up from her seat and marched towards their bedroom.

Mase followed behind her. "Don't touch my shit, Jada!!"

Jada ignored him. She flipped on the light switch and swung open the closet door. Jada ripped Mase's clothes off of the hangers and tossed them in his direction. Her rage had reached its peak.

"Stop that shit", warned Mase.

"Fuck You!" Jada said. She continued her tirade. Mase caught his flying wardrobe and threw them back in her direction. Jada tossed them back at him. "I hate you", she said.

"I hate you too!", he screamed back at her.

The couple was face to face. Nose to nose. Their lips touched and a passionate kiss ensued.

"I hate you, Mase", said Jada in between kisses.

Mase did not answer instead he lowered his lips to her neck and kissed.

"I love you, Mase", whispered Jada.

They began to undress each other. Mase lifted her up. Her body was warm, soft, and light. He carried her naked body onto their bed. They made love. They had sex, and then made love again. The argument was over. Tomorrow was another day. They fell asleep in each other's arms. It was 11:30 PM...

**Chapter 4**


Pieces of Life


Ms. Janice was a recovering alcoholic. She had been sober for 10 years now, but being sober did not change her life one bit. She still lived from check to check, her bills still continued to accumulate.

Ms. Janice was in her late 40s. She constantly worried about where her life was headed. Her good looks and sexy physique were rapidly disintegrating. She did not have any kids and her family was slim to none. She had been married in her younger days, but the marriage only lasted a year. Her ex-husband moved out of state after he filed for divorce. She never saw him again even so, she thought about him often.

Today is going to be different, Ms. Janice decided. She forced herself out of bed and got dressed. She looked at herself in the mirror and wondered how did 40 years go by so quick. She tried to recall her life before she quit drinking. Her thoughts were one big blur. She thought about her love life and how she moved from one relationship to the next. Ms. Janice even tried dating women for a while, but love never lasted.

Today is going to be different, she said to herself as she applied makeup to her aging face. After she finished, she called in to her job to inform them that she would not make it in today.

"Everything okay, Ms. Janice?" asked Lee the young manager at her job.

"I think I'm comin' down with a virus", Ms. Janice lied.

"Okay, Ms. Janice. I hope you feel better soon", said Lee.

Ms. Janice hung up the phone, grabbed her purse and walked out of her apartment door. She walked through the neighborhood where she had lived for most of our life. It was early morning, a few people stood around in groups. Some of those people were outside from the night before, others had awakened early morning to start off their day.

01/16/2015

Ms. Janice walked passed a group of young men shooting dice. "Hey, Ms. Janice", one of the young men said.

"Hey", said Ms. Janice. She could hear one of the young men comment on a how nice and plumb her ass looked. Ms. Janice smiled to herself and thought, I'm still fine. I still got it! Even though she did not feel like she still "had it" the compliment made her day. It was better than being ignored.

Ms. Janice made it to the cornerstore and went inside. The owner of the store, Mr. Gibson greeted her. "Good mornin', Ms. Janice." Mr. Gibson was a dirty old man who flirted with all of the women when his wife was not around.

"Good mornin', Mr. Gibson."

"What can I get from you?" Mr. Gibson asked while staring at Ms. Janice's breasts.

Ms. Janice pulled out her money from her purse. "Gimme a fifth of Southern Comfort and a box of Newport 100s."

"Ms. Janice, when you started drinkin' again?" Mr. Gibson asked with mock concern in his voice. Mr. Gibson could not take his eyes off of her lovely breasts.

"Mr. Gibson, I'm grown. I don't have to answer to nobody about when and why I drink."

"You right, Ms. Janice, you right." Mr. Gibson got the liquor and cigarettes. He rung up the total on his cash register and placed the items in a bag.

Ms. Janice paid. She grabbed her things and her change, she walked out of the store without saying another word.

She walked passed the young men shooting dice. She could feel their eyes on her. Ms. Janice twisted her hips extra hard. Her big butt aroused the young men. She heard the nasty comments they said amongst themselves. The nasty comments made Ms. Janice feel 10 years younger.

As she approached her apartment, her next-door neighbor Myrtle called out to her. "Hey Janice, girl. What you got in the bag?"

"None of your damn business", answered Ms. Janice.

Myrtle stared at Ms. Janice in disbelief. Myrtle rolled her eyes and slammed the door closed.

Ms. Janice entered her comfortable apartment, she fixed herself a big glass of ice and cracked open her drink. She poured the Southern Comfort over the ice, she listened as the ice crackled. She lit up a Newport and took a long gulp from our glass. She turned on the radio. Motown's greatest hits jammed through the speakers. Ms. Janice turned the volume up to the max and took another swallow of her drink.

Her body tingled. 10 years of sobriety vanished. Ms. Janice was ready to party! She was ready to have fun. She decided that life was too short to walk around stress and sober. Might as well go out with a bang, she thought to herself. She took a drag from a cigarette and sipped on her drink. The music school are soul, and from that point on, her life was launched into a different dimension.

**Chapter 5**


The Suffering of a Fool


Tyson Slaw was in a rut that he could not get out of. He was fed up with life. Tyson's life was one big dramatic cycle that he could not break.


Tyson's alarm clock buzzed at 6 AM. His common-law wife, Peaches opened up her eyes. "Do you want me to cook you some breakfast, bae?" Peaches asked.


Tyson hated the sound of her voice. In fact, he hated everything about Peaches. Everything except her sexy body and her bedroom skills.


"No bae, I'm okay. Go back to sleep", said Tyson.

Peaches tossed the covers off of herself, revealing her sexy body. "I hafta get them children up for school."

Tyson sat at the edge of the bed, admiring Peaches'body. Peaches'sexy body had yielded nine kids, and two of those kids were his. The other kids were from previous relationships and various baby daddys. Tyson met peaches at a club, 15 years earlier and as they say, the rest is history.

Tyson rubbed his head, he thought about the long day ahead of him. He was tired, but he got up and went into the bathroom to brush his teeth. He put on his work uniform and headed to the kitchen. His son, Tyson Jr. sat at the table eating breakfast.

"Good morning, son. Where's your brother?" Tyson asked the teen.

"I dunno", answered Tyson Jr. Tyson Jr. or TJ for short, stared at the television like a half asleep zombie.

Tyson went into the bedroom to look for his other son. The eight-year-old was sitting in his room, playing his new PlayStation 3.

"Brad, get off that game and go eat yo' breakfast", said Tyson.

Brad was his youngest son and also his favorite. Brad was the glue that kept Tyson and Peaches together. There were rumors around town that Brad was not his son, but Tyson ignore those rumors. He loved Brad more than anything.

"I'm not hungry, daddy", said Brad.

Tyson leaned over and kissed the youngster on his forehead. Tyson pressed the power button and turned the PlayStation off.

"Aww daddy, why you do that?" Brad asked.

"Because it's time for school, son", said Tyson. "Get your booksack and get ready."

Brad pouted but did as he was told.

Tyson went into the living room where Peaches was sitting on the couch, watching the news. "I packed your lunch, bae", said Peaches without looking away from the television.

"Thanks, bae", said Tyson. He glanced at her sexy body. His manhood began to rise. Peaches was sexy even while wearing baggy pajama pants. Tyson picked up his lunch and headed for the door.

"Tyson", Peaches yelled after him.

"What?"

"Do you want anything special for supper tonight?"

Tyson thought for a second. "Chicken in a brown gravy."

"Okay. Bye, bae."

"Bye daddy", said TJ.

"Bye daddy", said Brad.

"Bye", said Tyson as he walked out of the door.

Tyson climbed into his most prized possession, a 2004 Cadillac Escalade. Tyson turned his radio to a blues station. He drove out of the yard and headed for work. It was 6:45 AM. He was due for work in 15 minutes.

### 

Tyson Slaw arrived at his job with a smile on his face. He had been employed at Alpha- Vita for 20+ years. His job was his livelihood. His job was his home away from home. All the employees and supervisors knew him.

"Wassup, Tyson", an employee named Louis called out.

"What up, Louis."

Louis had been employed at Alpha - Vita for five years. He was young and ambitious. Louis secretly  vied for Tyson's position.Tyson knew this, so he kept a close eye on the young man. Tyson was a crew leader, a position that Louis would sell his soul to the devil to acquire.

"Tyson", Ol man Clay the supervisor, called out as soon as Tyson walked into the building.

"What the fuck you want, Ol' man?" Tyson asked jokingly.

Ol' man Clay smiled. He loved Tyson like a son. Tyson had saved the old man's job for years, and the old man was very greatful. "We got inspections coming up, so I need you to put these lazy mutha fuckas to work."

"Look Ol' man, I'm sick and tired of doin' yo' job. Don't you get paid to supervise?" Tyson said.

Ol' man Clay laughed. He knew that without Tyson, his job would have been gone a long time ago.

"You need me to do anything, Mr. Clay?" Louis asked. Louis was a kiss ass and Ol' man Clay knew this.

Ol' man Clay hated the young man, but he admired Louis' work ethic. "Whatever Tyson tells you to do, that's what you do", said Ol' man Clay.

Louis frowned. He wanted Tyson's position and he would stop at nothing to get it. My time will come, thought Louis to himself.

Tyson, the crew leader gave out orders and the workday proceeded. Tyson loved his job, he made enough money to pay his bills and take care of Peaches'demanding needs. Sometimes Tyson wondered if Peaches was with him strictly for the money.

### ###

Tyson drove home deep in thought. He stopped to the store and bought a case of beer and two packs of cigarettes for Peaches. He climbed back into his Cadillac Escalade and popped open a can of beer. A group of sexy girls passed by and honked the horn at him. Tyson honked back and smiled. Damn I wish I was single, he thought. He reminisced on his earlier life, when he had multiple women at his disposal.

Tyson was committed to Peaches, but he had doubts about her. He had heard rumors about Peaches' unfaithfulness, but he ignored the small talk. If he ever caught her in the act, he swore to himself that he would leave her with the quickness. He vowed that if he left Peaches, he would get himself a young tender 20-year-old. Tyson was in his early 50s and he constantly wondered how a 20-year-old piece of ass would feel. Young tight pussy is what he longed for, but for now he was stuck with Peaches. Peaches, was also in her early 50s. Peaches, who had nine kids from five different men, including himself.

Sometimes when he and Peaches had sex, Tyson would fantasize about Peaches taking dick from other men. It secretly turned him on.

Tyson spotted Peaches and her sister, Rose sitting outside as he drove slowly into his yard. He climbed out of his vehicle with the case of beer and the cigarettes in hand.

"Hey bae, how was work? Are those cigarettes for me?" Peaches asked. "I didn't cook yet."

"Well, what the fuck you been doin' all day", said Tyson.

Peaches'sister Rose laughed. Tyson did not like Rose. He knew that Rose cheated on her husband without shame, so Tyson's philosophy was that birds of a feather flock together.

"Aww bae, calm down and give me a beer. I been washin' clothes and cleanin' up", said Peaches.

"Yeah I bet, Peaches", said Tyson. He handed Peaches a beer and the two packs of smokes.

"Lemme get a beer, brother-in-law", said Rose.

Tyson rolled his eyes at Rose and handed her a brew. "What the fuck you doing here, Rose besides gossipin'?"

Rose laughed. She cracked open her beer, crossed her legs, and lit up a cigarette. Tyson stole a glance at Rose's coffee brown legs. Rose was sexy and a year younger than Peaches, but a whore just the same. Tyson wondered why did Rose's husband put up with her infidelities, but after staring at her body he immediately knew the answer. Rose was stacked. Big ass and nice legs was all a woman needed to have a man overlook her cheating ways.

Tyson grabbed a lounge chair and sat next to the women. Tyson listened as the sisters gossiped. He watched as the women sipped their beers and went on about who was fucking who, who was pregnant, and the life choices of their older children.

Tyson killed off his beer and popped open another can. "Peaches, where my kids at?"

"TJ is at football practice and Brad went to Rose's house. He left with my niece, Felicia", said Peaches.

Peaches was always getting rid of the kids and that pissed Tyson off. Peaches'other seven kids were all grown with kids of their own. The older kids all had their own homes, but they constantly came around like leeches asking for money. Money that Tyson had to dish out because they could never keep up with their bills.

Peaches had five daughters and two sons, not counting the last two boys which were

Tyson's.


Peaches and Rose began to gossip once again.


Tysons took a sip of his beer and said, "so when you plan on cookin'? I don't give

you money every week just for you to sit on yo' ass, you know."


"Bae, you hungry? I thought you was workin' late that's why I didn't start the food

yet", said Peaches.


"Well, I'm home now", said Tyson. He threw his empty can of beer on the ground

and reached for another.


"Look Tyson, don't start yo' shit. I need a break. I'm always cookin', cleanin',

washin' clothes. I feel like a got damn slave sometimes", said Peaches.


Rose laughed and grabbed another beer. She crossed her coffee brown legs and

waited for the drama to unfold.


"A slave!", Tyson shouted. "I'm the one goin' to work in bustin' my ass every day.

And you the one complainin'. Feel like I'm just payin' to fuck you!"

"Trust me, boo-boo. You not all that good", said Peaches.

Rose bust out laughing. Peaches had told her that Tyson was a good provider, but he was not at all good in bed.

Tyson gulped his beer down. "Oh yeah? I guess one of them niggas you had before me was better."

"Fuck you, Tyson. You know good bastard."

"No fuck you, Peaches. I'm startin' to feel sorry that I ever took you for my woman."

Tyson's words cut into Peaches like a two edged sword. She paused for a moment to regain her composure. "Well go back to yo sorry ass  first wife. You and her belong together because ya'll both ain't shit."

"Y'all need to stop that", said Rose even though she didn't mean it. Rose was enjoying the drama.

"Mutha fucka, if it wasn't for my kids I would have left yo sorry ass a long time ago", said Tyson pointing his finger at Peaches. It took every ounce of strength that he had not to strike her.

"Leave Tyson, I don't need you or yo sorry ass money. I'll put yo ass on child support."

"Fuck you and yo child support", said Tyson. He picked up what was left of his case of beer and headed towards the house.

"Y'all need to stop", said Rose even though she was laughing on the inside.

"Fuck him, sorry mutha fucka", said Peaches. "I know a lotta niggas who want this pussy."

Tyson turned around. "Well bitch, go give it to 'em!"

### #

Tyson laid next to Peaches in their bed, half asleep and naked. His belly was full. Peaches had cooked up a good meal. After eating, Peaches came into the bedroom where Tyson was laying and stripped off her clothes. She fucked him like a deranged woman. The sex only lasted five minutes, but Tyson was well satisfied. The couple never brought up the argument they had earlier.

For now, Tyson was satisfied. His belly was full and he had busted a nut. Tyson pulled back the blankets to admire Peaches' sexy, tall body. Peaches was in a deep sleep. He glanced at the alarm clock sitting on top of the dresser. Six more hours before he had to get up for work. He stared at the big bush of hair around Peaches' vagina. Tyson promised himself, that one day he was going to leave his no good common law wife. But for now, he was content. He decided to hold on as long as he could because Peaches had some good ass pussy!

**Chapter 6**


The Villian of Vermilion Parish


I am the biggest rapper in Abbeville, La. Scratch that, I'm the biggest rapper in Vermillion Parish. My success did not happen overnight. It took blood, sweat, tears, and many long nights in the studio. My music was finally being recognized. Everybody knew about the Iceman in the hood.


I had acquired the fame, but now all I was waiting on is that big payday! I hustled on the block until that big payday showed itself. A rapper ain't a rapper unless he has the perks that comes with the lifestyle. The cars, the clothes, the jewels, and the ho's. I am a rapper, a hustler, and a criminal. I love the lifestyle. My future was looking bright, but haters would do anything to stop my shine.


### #

"Ice, we need to start shootin' some videos, man. We can post them on YouTube and get some exposure", my producer Lil' Cut said. I had known Lil' Cut since high school, he was a computer nerd turned rap producer. Cut produced the dopest beats in the hood and he was partially responsible for my success.

I rolled up a blunt and lit it. "Find out who's doin' videos at a reasonable price."

"I already did", said Lil' Cut. "This lil' dude from Lafayette do some fire ass work. We need to get with him."

I passed the blunt to Cut and he greedily accepted it. Cut loved weed, he believed that weed enhanced his creative side. I loved weed too, but I smoked to relieve my stress. Hustlin' ain't a easy job and the stress of the streets can kill you.

I went through my rhyme pad and pulled out a new song that I had written. I built a cheap home studio inside my crib from money I made from hustlin'. I had a three-bedroom house that my Grandpops had left to me after he passed away. The house needed a little work but the rent was free. Lil' Cut slept over sometimes when we had a late night studio session. Lil' Cut and I were the dynamic duo. Michael Jackson and

Quincy Jones.


"We need about three more songs to finish this mixtape", said Lil' Cut. He passed

me the blunt.


I nodded my head and took a puff of the weed. "I gotcha covered, Cut. You know

what I'ma call this one?"


"What?"


"The Villian of Vermilion Parish."


Lil' Cut smiled. Cut didn't grow up in the hood, but he loved gangsta rap. He

loved to rebel against the system in any way possible. Cut's beats were sinister and

funky. His beats fit my rhymes like a glove. I rolled up another blunt and lit it. My cell

phone rang. It was my baby mama, Tee.


I answered. "What up, Tee."


"Don't what up me, nigga. I heard how you was flexin' at the club for them

bitches", said Tee.

Tee was always "hearing" shit about me. Tee was one fine ass Mutha fucka, but she was a complete drama queen. Every time she "heard" something about me, she needed more money for the baby. I didn't mind taking care of my child, I loved my son. But Tee used our son like a meal ticket and her childish ways pissed me off.

"Look Tee, I'm in the studio. What you want?"

"You always in the studio. Your son needs some Pampers. When are you gonna make some time for us?" Tee asked.

"I'll drop some money off tomorrow", I said. Before she could say another word, I hung up the phone. I didn't want Tee's drama to kill my vibe. I had to lay these songs.

Lil' Cut laughed. "Baby mama drama?"

"Yeah", I said, "you know how these bitches be."

We both laughed. Lil' Cut pulled up a dope track on his laptop. I went into the booth and put on the headphones. My studio booth was small, but I liked it that way. In my small booth, I felt a distance from the rest of the world. Nothing else mattered when I was in the booth laying a song. I put my heart and soul into my music.

It was 3 o'clock in the morning. Lil' Cut and I had laid down three songs. Two songs that I had written, and the last song I freestyled. We sat and listened as the songs playing through the speakers. I felt proud!

Lil' Cut bobbed his head to the music. "Man, niggas 'gon love this shit."

I smiled. Lil' Cut was not a yes man. He always gave his honest opinion on our songs. When he didn't like a song he would say, "it needs some work." Cut was a perfectionist like me. I guess that is why we worked together.

"I'm gonna mix these songs down and put in a few knickknacks, here and there", said Lil' Cut.

I checked my cell phone. I had a few missed calls from my customers. My mind switched from rapper to a hustler's mode. I had to get the money together to finance our video. "Alright Cut, I gotta go", I said.

"Where you goin', Ice? I need your opinion on this shit."

"I trust you, Cut. You got it from here. I have to get on my grind. Money is callin' plus I gotta drop Tee some cash."

Cut didn't agree with me selling drugs, but he knew it had to be done. Cut wasn't no d-boy but he wasn't no punk either. He loved to get into some gangsta shit, but he had no patience for hustling. Cut would rather go out and rob.

I left Cut in the studio and jumped into my old school Chevy. I reached for my pistol under the seat and placed it in my lap. I turned on my CD player and jammed some UGK. I drove through the hood like a wolf on the hunt. I was the Iceman, the ghetto star of Vermilion parish.

### 

I drove down MLK, searching for this kid named Slick Jack. Slick Jack owed me some money, $250. Jack had been dodging me. Word got around the hood that Slick said, fuck me, he wasn't paying. Every hustler knows that coming up short with money is a no- no.

I took a left at the first corner and spotted Slick Jack. He was with two other dudes, shooting dice. It was Slick Jack's roll so he didn't notice when my car pulled up. I placed my pistol in the waist of my pants. This was going to be a piece of cake.

"Hey Slick, where my money at?" I said in a loud voice.

I startled him. Slick Jack dropped the dice and looked at me with fear in his eyes. The two goons with him stuck out their chest and looked at me with mean eyes. But their attitudes changed when I pulled the pistol from my waist.

"Wassup Ice, what's that gun foe, homey?" Slick Jack asked as he stood up. " I'ma have yo' money sometimes next week."

"Naw Slick, you way past due. I want my money now", I said as I walked towards him. "My money or I'm takin' it out yo ass."

I could still see the fear in Slick Jack's eyes, but like every body in the hood he had a reputation to uphold. "I ain't got it right now, nigga. Now you can play around with that pistol, but you 'gon hafta kill..."

I slapped him with the pistol as hard as I could. Slick Jack fell to the ground with blood gushing from his face. I pointed the pistol at the two goons. They raised their hands up and backed away.

"Where my money, nigga?" I asked through gritted teeth.

"I told you, I ain't..."

I leaned over and struck him with the pistol again. Blood leaked like a faucet from Slick Jack's mouth. I stood over him and pointed the pistol inches away from his face. "Empty yo' pockets", I demanded. "Do it now before I kill yo ass."

Slick Jack emptied both pockets and placed two rolls of cash on the asphalt. I picked up the cash and counted it. $400. I counted out my $250 and stuffed it in my pocket. I threw the rest of the money back on the ground.

"You almost made me kill yo' ass over 250 measly dollars", I said as I waved my pistol and backed away towards my car.

Slick Jack bled heavily. Tears fell from his eyes, he was afraid now. Afraid of what I might do. I got into my car and drove off. One of Slick Jack's goons yelled out something as I drove away. I didn't care, I had my money. I turned up the volume on my radio and jammed some UGK. I was on my way to my next mission...

I had a meeting with Eli. Eli was one of the biggest suppliers in Abbeville. He moved product from Texas to Louisiana in large quantities. I did business with Eli because he was a straight up dude, and his prices were cheap. I pulled up to Eli's house and knocked on the door.

Eli opened up the door and smiled when he recognized me. "Come in, Ice. I've been waiting on you."

Eli was an older cat who like to keep his business quiet. He had told me that he was from Africa, but he didn't have an African accent. People from the hood feared Eli. Some say that he was a straight up killer. I had never witnessed Eli's murderous side, nor would I want too.

I entered Eli's house. The smell of marijuana was heavy in the air. Eli passed me a blunt and sat his tall frame down on his plush sofa. "Take a seat, Ice."

I sat down and took a long pull of the blunt. I always kept my eyes opened around Eli. I just didn't trust him. I passed the blunt back to Eli.

A half naked, tall, yellow Amazon entered the room. "Eli, when you comin' to bed. I wanna fuck", she said.

I tried not to stare at her out of respect for Eli, but my eyes refused to look away.

Eli laughed. "I'll be there in a few minutes, baby. I'm talking some business with my man, Ice."

The Amazon never looked my way.

"Hurry up, baby. I'm horny", she said as she left the room. Her big yellow ass bounced as she walked away.

"Bitches", said Eli, "can't live with them, can't live without them."

I nodded my head in agreement. "So what you got for me, Eli?" I asked. I wanted to get straight down to business.

Eli took a hit of the blunt. "I have a business proposition for you. How's the music going? Ya know, I'm still jammin' to your last mixtape."

"The music is goin' good. We got another mixtape being made right now as we speak. What kind of business you talkin' 'bout, Eli?"

Eli stared me down with his bloodshot eyes. "A 187."

I had never taken a life before, not because I wouldn't it just never came down to that. In the game I played, I knew that murder came along with the territory.

Eli continued, "I have a snitch problem. A nigga been singing about my business to the po-po's. I need him eliminated.

I hated snitches. Snitches fucked up the hustling game. "How much we talking?"

" 10 gees now and 10 gees when the job is finished", answered Eli.

20 gees sounded good in my pocket. I would have enough money for the video shoot and some money left over. I looked into Eli's bloodshot eyes and said, "I'm down."

Eli smiled a wicked smile. He rose up from the sofa and went into his bedroom. He came back with a stack of cash. He threw the money in my lap. I held the money in my hands. Cold hard cash, bloodmoney.

"Ice", said Eli pointing his long slender finger at me. "I don't have to tell you what this means, and I know I don't have to tell you don't fuck with my money."

"Eli, just give me the info and consider it done."

Eli smiled again and told me what I needed to know.

### 

It was 5:30 in the morning when I made it toTee's house. Tee was wide awake.

"Where's my son?" I asked when I walked through the door.

"I just put him to sleep. That son of yours is a handful", said Tee.

Tee was wearing a short, see- through nightgown. I admired her body as she pranced around. She was in a good mood and I was glad. I had a lot on my mind and I didn't feel like arguing. I took my shirt off and tossed it on the sofa.

"You got some weed?" Tee asked.

I pulled out a half ounce of weed from my pocket and tossed it to her. "Damn Ice, all you got is some reggie. Where's the purp?"

I didn't answer her. I was scheming on a murder. Life is a hustle and I was the ultimate hustler. Tee rolled up some blunts. We sat down and talked while we smoked...

**Chapter 7**

Ghetto Queen

Connie Breaux pushed her new BMW through traffic. She cursed as she nearly got sideswiped by some joker driving an old school Chevy.

Connie had it going on. She was conceited and self-centered, but beautiful all the same. She could not go anywhere without some man (or woman) admiring her beauty. Connie stopped at the red light. She fixed her lipstick as she waited for the light to change. A horn honked on the side of her. She looked. It was two guys in a convertible Corvette.

"Hey baby, what's your name?" asked the passenger.

Connie rolled her eyes and looked away. It's always the passenger trying to holla, she thought. The horn honked again. Connie eased up her BMW. The Corvette eased up alongside her.

"Baby, let me get your number", the driver of the Corvette said.

Connie rolled her eyes and said, " nigga, I got a man." The light turned green. Connie pushed down on her accelerator and sped off.

" Fuck you, bitch", the passenger said.

Niggas, Connie thought. She headed home. Once she made it home, she took out her shopping bags from the back seat of the car. Connie was the most popular girl in the neighborhood. Every guy wanted her and the women envied her style.

"Hey Connie", someone called out.

Connie spun around. It was her best friend, Lakeisha. "Wassup, Keish?"

Lakeisha was short and overweight. Connie and Lakeisha had known each other since kindergarten. Lakeisha admired Connie's hustle, as a matter of fact she looked up to Connie.

"Why you didn't tell me you was going shoppin', bitch?" Lakeisha asked with her hands on her thick hips.

Connie smacked her lips. " Keish, you know yo' lazy ass don't get up tell after 12 o'clock."

"You sho' is right."

The girls laughed.

"What you went get?" Lakeisha asked.

"Girl, I found those shoes that Beyoncé had on in her new video", said Connie.

The girls made small talk as they walked through the buildings of their project apartment.

"Girl, while you was gone the police ran up on Jalen", said Lakeisha.

"Girl, you lie. Did they arrest him?" Connie asked with concern in her voice.

"No."

Connie was relieved. Connie loved Jalen and she did not want any harm to come to him even though he was a no good dog.

As they neared Connie's apartment, a young woman appeared. The woman was pretty and slim with long flowing hair. Her name was Peanut, Connie's arch rival. Peanut was walking alongside her little girl. A little girl who was supposed to be Jalen's daughter.

Peanut looked at Connie and rolled her eyes. Peanut rubbed her fingers across a shining new gold necklace that she was wearing. Connie lifted up her left hand revealing the diamond ring she was wearing. The two women glared at each other for a second and then rolled their eyes at each other.

Connie took out her keys and opened her apartment door.

"That Peanut ain't nothin' but a ho'", Lakeisha said after Peanut was well out of hearing range.

"Yeah, that bitch think Jalen love her, but all he doin' is using her", said Connie.

Once in the apartment, Connie threw her bags on the couch and kicked out of her shoes. Her apartment was nice and clean and it smelled of strawberries. Connie was one of the few girls in the projects who kept her apartment tidy.

Lakeisha sat down on the love seat, pulled out a blunt from her pocket, and lit it up. "Gimme a ashtray", she said to Connie.

Connie went into the kitchen to get and ashtray. "Hold up Keish, let me light up some incense in case them laws come runnin' over here looking for Jalen again."

Connie lit up two exotic smelling incense. A sweet aroma filled the air. Lakeisha passed the blunt to Connie. Connie took a long hard hit. Connie loved to smoke weed, weed calmed her nerves. You gotta have something to calm your nerves dealing with these messy mutha fuckas in the projects, Connie thought.

Connie exhaled the smoke. "You think Jalen still fuckin' Peanut?" Connie asked Lakeisha.

Lakeisha took the blunt back when Connie passed it to her. "Knowin' how no good Jalen is, prolly so."

Connie thought hard about what Lakeisha said, and in her heart she knew that her friend was telling the truth.

### 

01/16/2015

Connie and Lakeisha smoked three blunts, back-to-back.

"Girl, I'm high as hell", said Lakeisha.

Connie ran her fingers through her long weave. A habit, she often did when she got high. "Girl, me too."

"My cousin O'Shea asked about you", said Lakeisha.

O'Shea was Connie's first love. They had dated all through high school. The two were suppose to go off to college together, but they grew apart. And then Connie met Jalen. "What he been up to?" Connie asked before she could stop herself.

"He still in Atlanta. He about to graduate, he gonna be an engineer", said Lakeisha. Lakeisha liked to rub her cousin O'Shea's success in Connie's face.

"For real", Connie said running her fingers through her weave. She was supposed to be there by O'Shea's side. Instead, she was stuck in the projects. Stuck dealing with Jalen's trifling ass. Her life had took on a whole different meaning. She thought for a second about what could have been.

A loud knock at the door startled the girls. Paranoia had set in. Connie knew that it had to be the police looking for Jalen. She rose up from her seat and snatched the air freshener off the counter. Lakeisha shifted in her seat. The knock came again, louder this time.

"Opened the door, Connie", hissed Lakeisha.

Connie went to the door and prepared for the worst. She opened the door and breathed a sigh of relief. It was her next-door neighbor, Miss Jackson. "Damn Ms. Jackson, I thought you was the police", said Connie.

"I'm sorry to scare you, my baby", the older lady said. Miss Jackson was always coming over to borrow sugar or ketchup, or to drop off a plate of food. Ms. Jackson was the neighborhood cook. Everyone in the projects loved her cooking. "Connie", said Ms. Jackson with a worried look on her face. "I don't know how to tell you this, so I'll just say it. Jalen got shot."

Connie's heart dropped. She was still high and for a moment she thought her mind was playing tricks on her. "Ms. Jackson, are you sure? Is he alive? Is he dead?"

"I dunno, baby. My son John just called and told me. He told me to come and let you know. Somethin' about Jalen and another boy got into it over a dice game. The cops got the road blocked off on MLK", said Ms. Jackson.

Connie tried to pull herself together. Lakeisha was up on her feet now. "Let's go see", said Lakeisha.

"Oh, thank you, Ms. Jackson", said Connie. She slammed the door shut. Her mind was spinning. Connie grabbed her keys and headed out of the door, without her shoes. Lakeisha followed behind her.

The girls jumped in the car and headed towards MLK. From a block away, the girls could see police cars with their lights on. A crowd walked toward the scene where the yellow tape was placed. Connie sped to the scene. She prayed and hoped that it was not Jalen. Maybe it was a case of mistaken identity, she thought. Once she got close to the scene, she parked to the side of the road, yanked her car door open, and jumped out.

"Hol' up, Connie", said Lakeisha trying to keep up.

Connie ignored Lakeisha and darted toward the yellow tape. She spotted a body laying on the road with blood flowing like a river. Was it Jalen? Connie recognized the dark blue Jordans that Jalen was wearing earlier that day. Her heart dropped. She was about to cross the yellow tape, but a police officer grabbed her. " Lemme go!" Connie

screamed.

"No, Jalen, no!" Lakeisha screamed in tears.

Connie tried to fight the officers grip, but he was strong as an ox.

" Jalen... Jalen! Jalen!" Connie screamed as if Jalen would get up and answer

her.

The crowd thickened. Everyone wanted to see the bloody body that was

sprawled on the street. It was another day and another death in the projects. Connie

screamed and cried until she passed out. But no matter what she did, it would not bring

Jalen back.

**Chapter 8**


Cruel World


The weight of the world was on his shoulders.


Bobby Winters rose out of his bed to face another day in his cruel reality. Bobby's pregnant wife, Mary was still asleep. He listened as Mary snored lightly. Mary's snoring was music to his ears.


Body went into the kitchen and put on a pot of coffee. The coffee container was low. As a matter of fact, the house was low on everything. Low on sugar, low on canned goods, low on rice, and low on meat. Bobby tried not to think about it as the aroma of coffee filled the air.


When the coffee finished, Bobby fixed himself a large cup and lit up a cigarette. He had three smokes left. Low on cigarettes, he made a mental note to himself. Bobby opened up his notepad which contained possible job contacts. He had to find a job soon. His family was depending on him.

Bobby thought about his seven-year-old daughter. He loved the child with all of his heart. It was a hurting feeling not being able to take little Bobbi out to McDonald's. His wife Mary was eight months pregnant with their second child. The pressure was mounting.

Bobby stared at the three job contacts written in his notepad. He had to find a job, today. He could not take no for an answer. Bobby went into the living room and turned on the television. He sipped on his coffee and viewed the news. The same ol' bullshit. A war in Syria. Angela Jolie had a new movie coming out. David Bowie had a new album on the way. All Bullshit! Where are the jobs? Bobby thought to himself.

Bobby was disgusted. He went back into the kitchen and lit up another cigarette. Two smokes left. Bobby felt like a fly buzzing on a large piece of shit. The bills were piling up and there was nothing he could do about it. He was watching his whole world unravel right before his face.

# # #

01/16/2015

"Baby, stop worryin'. Something is going to turn up. The good Lord is only testing you", said Mary.

Bobby looked at Mary with stern eyes. He wanted to tell her about the harsh realities of the world. He wanted to tell her that there was no God, but when he looked into her beautiful eyes he decided against it. "Thanks baby, Lord knows I could use the encouragement."

Mary smiled. She loved her husband. She had faith in him. The couple had been married for five years. Some of those years were very trying mostly because of their financial situation. But Bobby Winters always fought to make things right. As of late, Bobby was starting to lose hope. The reality of life had beaten him into submission. Long gone was the twinkle of fun in his eyes. His stare was now hard and mistrusting. Mary prayed every night for her husband to find a job.

Bobby ate breakfast and got dressed. He kissed little Bobbi on her forehead. The little girl smiled. "Daddy, I need a new bike."

"I'll get you one, just give Daddy a little time", said Bobby.

"How much time, Daddy?" asked little Bobbi. She was a curious little girl. She did not understand the struggles that her father was facing. Little Bobbi's question touched him mainly because he did not have a definite answer. And like any good father, he wanted to give his child the world.

"Bobbi, stop bothering your Daddy. He said he gonna get it, now be patient and finish your breakfast", said Mary.

The little girl scoffed and stuffed her mouth with a full spoon of oatmeal.

Bobbi kissed Mary on the lips and rubbed her pregnant belly. "Don't be so hard on her, Mary. She was only asking."

"You have her spoiled", said Mary, "you have us both spoiled. Your a good man, Bobby Winters and I'm proud to be Mrs. Winters."

Mary's words stirred something inside of his soul. Bobby felt like a new man. He walked out the front door with a smile on his face. He was ready to battle another day, in this cruel world!

**Chapter 9**


Victory & Defeat


Angelo had the reputation of a tough kid. He was well known in the streets of Abbeville. Angelo never let his rep go to his head. He knew that any moment his reputation could be jeopardized. He had seen it happen to others, many times.

Angelo walked the streets, stone faced and ready for action. He was a street nigga, at least that is what everyone else labeled him. Angelo learned at an early age that violence was respected and weakness was not tolerated. That's just the way things were. That's the way it has always been in the streets of Abbeville. Angelo did not like the way things were, but he accepted and adjusted to it.

"Hey, Angelo", a group of girls called out as they walked by. You could hear the admiration in their voices.

Being admired by the girls made Angelo feel good. "Hey", he said as he walked passed the girls trying to hold back a smile. Any other day, Angelo would stop and humor the girls, but today he was on a mission.

He wanted to stay focused on what he had to do. Angelo heard one of the girls say, "girl, he so fine." Angelo smiled inside. He wondered why the girls thought he was "so fine". He did not feel fine. He felt like an animal trapped in the jungle trying to survive.

Angelo continued walking. As he walked toward his destination, he could feel the tension in his body.

# # #

"I heard you been lookin' for me", said Luke. Luke was another tough kid from the neighborhood. Luke was always looking for trouble, as a matter of fact he thrived for it.

Luke had been to reform school twice, and he did not care if he went back. Luke had nothing to live for but his neighborhood.

Angelo looked Luke square in the eyes. "Yeah, I've been looking for you."

Luke smiled with evilness in his eyes. Luke was with two of his partners. The two kids looked up to Luke more out of fear than friendship.

Angelo knew the other two kids, but he did not know their names. Angelo wondered if he should have brought some of his crew. It was a slight possibility that he could get jumped. Even though the odds were against him, Angelo showed not a hint of fear.

"You mus' be comin' to get yo' ass kicked", said Luke's dark skinned sidekick.

"Naw, he must be comin' to beg for mercy", said Luke's light-skinned sidekick.

Angelo did not utter a word. He focused his eyes on Luke. Luke's face was stone, he had the face of a killer. Luke wanted to rip Angelo from limb to limb. Luke was not an intelligent kid, but he knew that Angelo was not a pushover. He had heard about Angelo's many victories all over the hood.

"Make yo' move, punk", said Luke coldly.

Angelo wanted to tear into Luke, but he knew that he had to be cautious. Luke's two sidekicks did not look tough at all, but they would sneak in punches if given the chance.

"Hey! We got a problem over here!" someone shouted.

The voice was familiar to Angelo's ears. Angelo did not turn around, but he could see someone approaching from the corner of his eyes. It was Kendall, Angelo's first cousin.

"What up, cuz. You got a problem with these fake ass niggas?" Kendall asked, staring hard at Luke and his crew.

Angelo smiled for a second and then regained his composure. He saw hesitation in the other boys now that the odds were slightly even. "I just need you to watch my back, so I can give one of these clowns a beat down", said Angelo to Kendall.

"No problem, cuz", said Kendall. Kendall loved to fight. Fighting was one of his many joys of life.

Angelo and Luke squared off and circled each other like two gladiators ready to fight to the death. Luke threw a wild right hook. Angelo dodged it. Angelo was focused on his enemy, but he could feel a crowd forming around him.

"Get that nigga, cuz!", Kendall shouted.

Luke threw a left jab. The punch landed and hit Angelo in the bridge of the nose. Angelo felt blood trickling down to his mouth. He could taste the salty flavor of blood. Luke smiled and then moved in for the kill, throwing punches in bunches. Angelo remained calm and kept his guards up. He blocked the first haymaker. The second punch grazed his jaw. And then Angelo saw his chance. He let go an uppercut like his Uncle Paul had taught him. The punch was loud like a shotgun blast. Luke looked surprised and confused all at once. He slumped to the ground like a sack of potatoes.

"That's how you do it, cuz", said Kendall with his hands in the air.

Angelo looked around. A great deal of people had crowded around to see the fight. Luke's sidekicks scurried away like squirrels. The girls that Angelo had spoken to earlier crowded around him touching his face. "You all right, Angelo?" asked one of the girls. She had big breasts and a pretty face.

"Yeah, I'm all right", said Angelo.

Angelo looked down at Luke who was still knocked out. Kendall patted Angelo on the back. Another victorious fight. But Angelo knew that in life a day would come when he would lose. But until that day, he was going to enjoy his victory.

**Chapter 10**

Wendy & Wes

Anticipation burned in her heart like a blazing fire. A year had passed since she had any physical contact with him. She was longing to hold him, kiss him, to touch him. He was the love of her life. Her loyalty and faithfulness would prove her love for him. She had not had any sexual contact with any other because she only desired to have him.

It was 12 AM. Wendy sat on the hood of her car waiting patiently. For the past year, Wendy prayed every night for this moment. She was dressed to impress. Wendy lit up a cigarette and puffed slowly, making sure that she did not mess up her lipstick. She gazed at the gates of the Vermilion parish jail and wondered how did her man survive in such a place. She was tempted many times during her weekend visits to bring a gun and spring him out. But luckily, she remained patient because tonight her love would be a free man.

After a year of living in the stinky rotten Vermilion parish jail, he was about to be released. He had fantasized many nights about holding his lady love in his arms, but now his dream would be a reality. He promised himself that he would never allow himself to be locked up again.

He gave all of his belongings to his cell mate, Red. Red had six more months before he would be granted his freedom. "Look me up when you get out", he told Red as the guard opened up the cell.

"Good luck, my nigga and keep your nose clean", said Red with a smile.

The two friends shook hands.

As he walked out of his cell to his freedom his heart picked up pace. After being locked up for a year, freedom was a foreign feeling to him.

Wes breathed in the midnight air as he walked toward the exit of the iron gates. He smiled at the moon and admired the stars. Freedom felt strange after being confined to steel bars. Wes became excited when he noticed the silhouette of a tall female. He could tell that she was beautiful even though he could not see her face. Her movements were graceful and regal. Wes picked up the pace.

"Wes, is that you?" the female figure called out.

Wes got a whiff of her sweet perfume and the smell immediately aroused him. He had dreamed about her aroma many nights, while asleep in his bunk. Without answering, he rushed into her. He hugged her and kissed her sweet lips. Her body was soft and warm. He wanted to hold her forever.

Wendy cried tears of joy. Wes wiped her tears away and said, "no more cryin', baby. Everything is going to be okay from now on."

Wendy smiled through her tears. "I know, baby. This is the start of a new beginning."

"Let's get outta here before they change their mind and lock me up again", said Wes.

Wendy and Wes jumped into their vehicle and drove away in the darkness. Leaving the nightmare of his incarceration far behind them.

# # #

01/16/2015

Wes and Wendy laid together in their plush bed wrapped in each other's arms, naked. Wes woke up confused about his surroundings. He looked down at Wendy's beautiful naked body and a smile came over his face. He held her tight. Wendy opened up her eyes and kissed him softly on the neck.

The morning sunlight illuminated through the window. Life and love had granted the couple another chance at happiness, so they relished In the moment.

"Baby, would you like me to fix you some breakfast?" Wendy asked.

Wes'mouth watered. After a year of eating jail food, he was ready to enjoy some good home cooking. "Yeah baby, that sounds good."

Wendy got out of bed, put on her robe, and headed towards the kitchen. Wes went into the bathroom and took a hot shower. He let the hot water run over his muscular body while he contemplated his next move. Finding a job was out of the question. Wes was a convicted felon, and he could not endure the humiliation of rejection.

Wes got out of the shower, got dressed, and walked into the kitchen. The aroma made his stomach growl. Eggs, bacon, biscuits, pancakes, and sausage. Wendy had done it up! The couple sat at the kitchen table eating and conversation.

"As soon as you find a job, we 'gon save up some money and move outta Abbeville", said Wendy nibbling at her food.

Wes did not answer.

"Wes, did you hear me?"

"Wendy, I've been thinkin'..."

"Thinkin' 'bout what, Wes?"

"I'll tell you if you let me finish, got dammit. I'm on parole and you know it's gonna be hard as hell for me to find a job", he said. "I got a plan that gonna get us outta here quick."

Wendy shook her head and rolled her eyes. "Look Wes, I'm not going for it. I'm so done with the street life and I'm done with jail visits. For now on, we 'gon work for what we want like every other law abiding citizen."

Wendy's words angered him. Wes slammed his fork down and stared at Wendy with cold eyes. "Law-abiding citizens, huh? Wendy, you don't know shit! I thought you was a smart girl. We ain't no citizens, baby especially here in Vermilion parish. We ain't nothin' but niggas to them! I'm a criminal, who in the hell is gonna hire my black ass!"

Wendy felt his anger. She could feel his pain, but she loved Wes and did not want him to go back to jail. Wendy began to weep.

Wes' attitude changed when he noticed the tears falling down her face. "I'm sorry, baby." He reached across the table and placed her hands in his. "Let's not talk about our situation right now. Let's just enjoy the moment, I love you."

"I love you too, Wes."

Wes leaned over the table and kissed her soft thick lips. They went back to eating breakfast. Wes loved Wendy. She was a good woman and he wanted to give her the world. He did not care what he had to do to give it to her. Wes enjoyed the taste of the bacon and eggs while he schemed on a master plan.

### 

01/16/2015

Three months had passed since Wes' release from jail. Staying free had proved to be more challenging than surviving on the inside. Wendy tried to encourage Wes and keep his mind off of crime. But crime as Wes knew it, was his only way out...

"Where'd you get that money from?" asked Wendy. She had arrived home from working a 12 hour shift at the nursing home.

Wes looked up from the table where he was counting a pile of cash. "I robbed a nigga."

"Wes, you promised you wouldn't do nothin' crazy!"

"Baby, if this is crazy", said Wes picking up a handful of cash. "Call me insane! I made $2500 in five minutes."

Wendy looked at the money. The money seemed to call her name. For the last few months, the couple had been struggling to make ends meet. It had been a while since Wendy enjoyed the benefits of an all out shopping spree. Maybe Wes was on to something, Wendy thought.

"What's my cut?" Wendy asked.

Wes stood up, embraced Wendy and kissed her on the lips. "We split everything 50-50. Bonnie and Clyde."

Wendy smiled. "No, Wendy and Wes. Now let's go shopping."

"Let's go", said Wes, "anything for my Queen."

A loud knock at the door startled the couple out of their moment of happiness. Wes tensed up and pulled out a chrome plated revolver from his waist.

"Wes, where did you get that from?" asked Wendy.

Wes motioned for her to be silent. He went to the front door and swung it open, with his weapon in hand.

"Hey man, this is how you treat an old friend?" Red asked with his hands in the air.

Wes smiled when he recognized his old cellmate. "Red, come in. You out already?" Wes put his gun in the waist of his baggy pants.

"Yeah, they let me out early for good behavior", said Red as he entered the house.

"Wendy, I got somebody I want you to meet. This is Red. You know my partner I was tellin' you about", said Wes.

Wendy lit up a cigarette and breathed a sigh of relief. "How you doin', Red?"

"Nice to meet you, Wendy. Wes told me a lot about you", said Red. Red looked at the cash piled up on the table. "Man, what da fuck you been doin' out here?" Red asked Wes.

"Robbin'", answered Wes.

"Robbin'?"

"Yeah, robbin'."

"I'll let you guys catch up on old times. I'm going take a shower", said Wendy. "I smell like old people." She turned to Wes and asked, "we still going shoppin', huh?"

"Of course, baby", said Wes.

     

Wendy left the room excited. She thought about what she was going to buy as she headed to the bathroom.

"Have a seat, Red", said Wes as he gathered up the cash from the table and placed it in a black sack.

Red sat across from Wes, admiring the greenbacks.

"I need a partner, Red", said Wes getting straight to the point.

"I'm down, Wes. I've been havin' nothin' but bad luck since I've been free. I can't find a job and my ol' gal been trippin'. I've been trying to sell a lil' reefer, but so many niggas on the corner trying to hustle it's ridiculous."

Wes knew the pain of being broke all to well. "I have an answer to all your problems, Red."

"Yeah, wassup?"

"Robbin' a bank."

Wes, what the fuck you talkin' about. Robbin' banks man, that's Fed time."

"It's only Fed time if you get caught and I don't plan on going back to prison. I've been scopin' shit out. We hit this bank on Main Street. In and out, about 100 grand easy in less than five minutes."

Red smiled. Red was a criminal at heart and he loved the thrill of committing crimes. "I'm down."

Wes reached into his money sack and pulled out three crisp $100 bills. He tossed the bills to Red. Red took the cash and placed it in his pocket.

"Come by tomorrow and we'll discuss the specifics", said Wes.

Wendy entered the kitchen, dressed to impress. She loved fashion and was somewhat of a diva. "You ready to go, Wes?"

"Yeah baby, let's do it."

Red rose up from his seat and headed towards the door. "I'll holla at you tomorrow."

All right, dawg", said Wes.

Wes and Wendy got into their vehicle, it had been a long time since they had been on a shopping spree. Wes felt good. Wendy was his Queen and she deserved the best. By any means necessary, he promised that he was going to give it to her. "Baby."

"What?" Wendy asked with a bright smile on her face.

"I love you."

"I love you too, Mr. Wes."

Wes leaned over and kissed Wendy on the cheek as they sped into the traffic.

### 

Wendy maneuvered the stolen blue Chevy towards Main Street. She was nervous, but she tried not to show it. She could not believe that she had let Wes talk her into this. Wes sat in the passenger seat with a 9 mm in his lap.

Wes went over the plan in his head, over and over again. He could not fail because failure would land him back in the slammer. He hated having Wendy involved, but there was no one else he could trust.

Red sat in the backseat. Red was wired up. He had sniffed a few lines of coke to even out his nerves. Red felt no fear. He would kill anyone who got in his way especially if they tried to jeopardize his freedom. Red slipped on his black gloves. He was ready to raise hell!

The trio's quest for a better life depended on this heist. They all knew that it was "do or die time".

Wes cocked his weapon. "Okay, we two blocks away", Wes turned around to face Red. "You ready, nigga?"

"Let's make it happen", said Red with a grimacing look on his face. Red held onto his gun, itching to pull the trigger.

Wendy drove the Chevy onto the curb on the side of the bank. Her hands began to shake. This is it, no turning back, she thought. Wes took a hold of her arm and pulled her close to him. He kissed her gently. "Keep the engine runnin'. Everything is gonna be okay", said Wes. Wendy shook her head in agreement. Tears escaped her eyes before she could stop them.

Wes and Red pulled their ski masks down over their faces. They opened up the car doors, and headed out to their suicide mission. "Five minutes, baby. We'll be in and out in five minutes", were the last words Wes spoke to her...

www.ingramcontent.com/pod-product-compliance
Lightning Source LLC
Chambersburg PA
CBHW080001180726
48002CB00020B/2915